Daddy's 1st Dance

A Kid's Guide to Overcoming Anxiety

Written by Amanda Lynch, Hazy Lynch, and Primrose Lynch
Art by Bonnie Lemaire

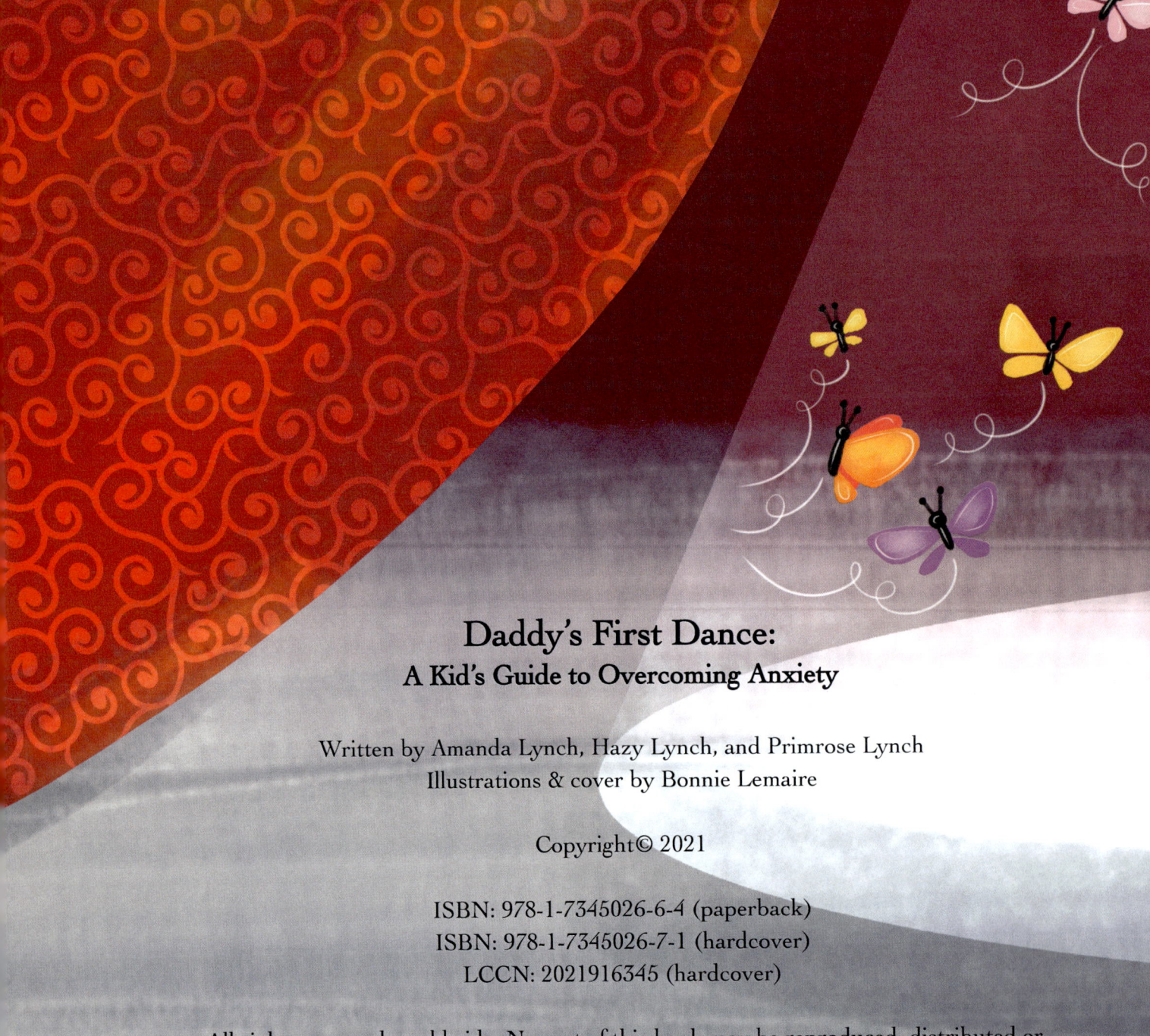

Daddy's First Dance:
A Kid's Guide to Overcoming Anxiety

Written by Amanda Lynch, Hazy Lynch, and Primrose Lynch
Illustrations & cover by Bonnie Lemaire

Copyright© 2021

ISBN: 978-1-7345026-6-4 (paperback)
ISBN: 978-1-7345026-7-1 (hardcover)
LCCN: 2021916345 (hardcover)

All rights reserved worldwide. No part of this book may be reproduced, distributed or transmitted in any form or by any means without the prior written permission of the author, except in the case of brief quotations embodied in critical reviews.

To our Daddy, Papas, Pop Pop, and Grindaddy.

Thank you for always showing up as your best selves for us.

We love you.

Hazy and Rosie

Dear parents,

Your child's brain rapidly develops between conception and age six. In fact, most of your child's brain development occurs in the earliest parts of life. A nutritious diet and positive experiences and relationships are crucial for healthy brain development.

By reading to, playing with, and introducing breathwork to your child, you can help him or her develop healthy, brain-boosting habits that last a lifetime. It's never too early (or too late) to start talking to your child about the developing brain and how it works.

Sometimes when we are stressed, we're unable to regulate our emotions. Meditation, breathwork, and yoga are mindfulness tools that help kids think before they act. These tools may help our brains and bodies calm down when we are feeling anxious or overwhelmed.

These strategies also work great for adults. This book is filled with simple, age-appropriate ways to breathe through "big feelings".

For additional information, activities, and resources, check out the best-selling book *The Mindfulness Room* and rethinkingresiliency.com.

My name is Stella Bean Brown, and I'm a ballerina.
I love ballet.

Every Saturday morning, my daddy takes me to ballet class.

I really love my daddy.

This year he's dancing in the dads' dance at my ballet recital.

I'm so excited, but my daddy is really nervous!

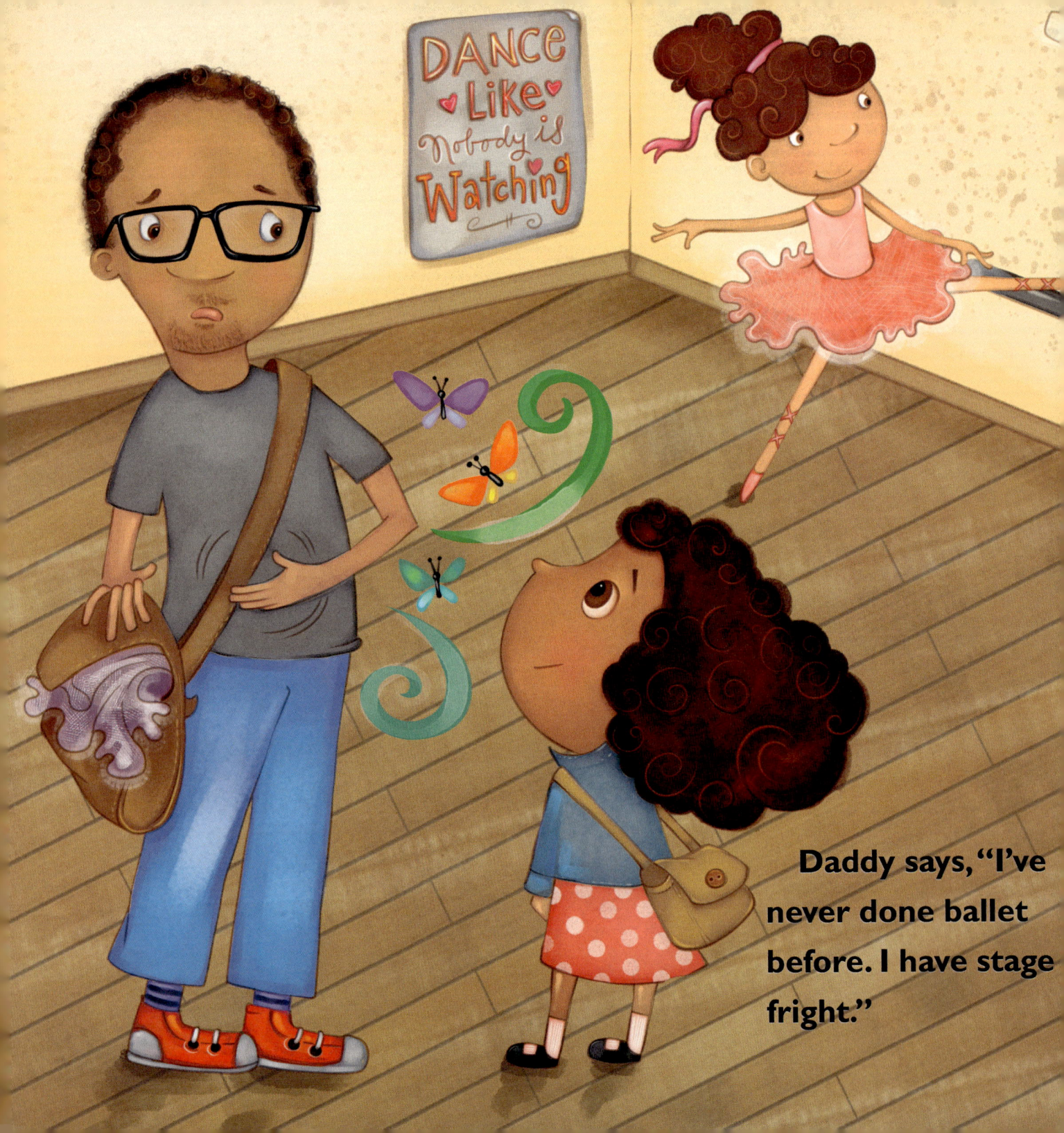

Daddy says, "I've never done ballet before. I have stage fright."

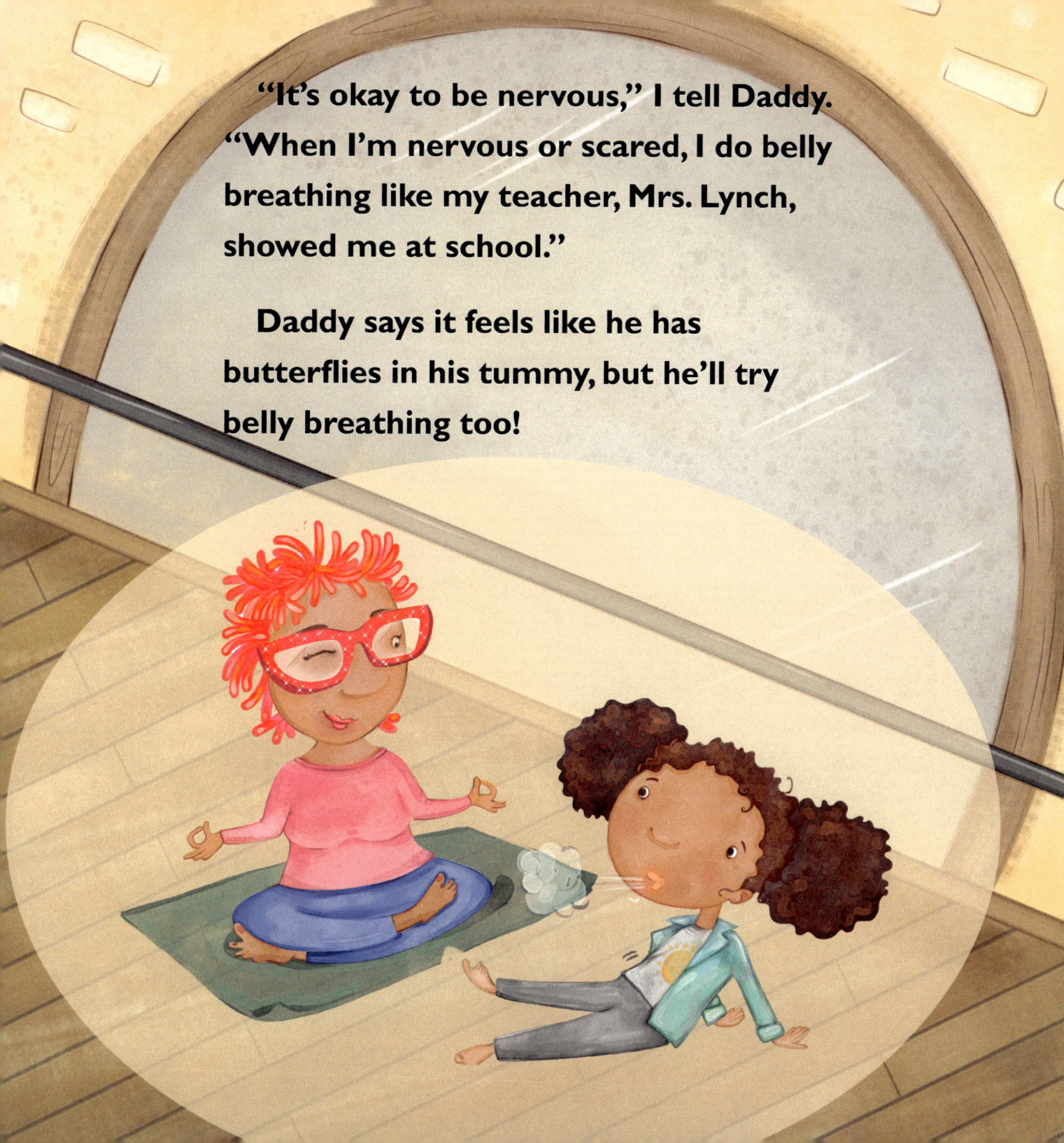

"It's okay to be nervous," I tell Daddy. "When I'm nervous or scared, I do belly breathing like my teacher, Mrs. Lynch, showed me at school."

Daddy says it feels like he has butterflies in his tummy, but he'll try belly breathing too!

For three whole months, my daddy goes to dance rehearsals every weekend with all the other dads.

Sometimes, I watch from the dance studio lobby.

Sometimes, we practice together at home.

Sometimes, I help him with his combinations.

I practice a few deep belly breaths with Daddy before each rehearsal until the butterflies in his tummy go away.

I see Daddy taking deep breaths when he's on the phone for work. He takes deep breaths when we are stuck in traffic on the way to school.

Sometimes, he takes really deep breaths with his eyes closed when he's at rehearsal, just like we practiced at home. That makes me smile!

On the day of the recital, Daddy looks really scared. I remind him to find his breath and imagine he's watching the butterflies from his tummy float away into the sky.

Backstage, he smiles at me just before the music starts for his turn to go on.

Daddy closes his eyes and takes a few deep breaths.

Breathe in deeply for four counts.

Breathe out slowly for four counts.

Watch the butterflies float away.

Plié, relevé, plié, sauté. Plié, relevé, plié, sauté.

All the dads do a great job, and my daddy doesn't miss a beat.

Everyone gets scared sometimes, even daddies.

But we breathe in, we breathe out, and we dance on.

BREATHWORK SCRIPTS

Belly Breathing

You are always breathing. Though your breath flows in and out, it's always with you. You can control your breathing and return to it at any time. Remember you are working to make your brain stronger!

Steps

Get into a comfy position. You can stand, sit, or lie down. You may use a pillow, mat, cushion, or chair. Just make sure you're comfortable.

Close your eyes if that feels okay, or you can look at the tip of your nose. Allow yourself to relax.

Bring your attention and awareness to your belly. As you breathe in, inflate your belly like a beach ball or balloon.

Relax your tummy on your exhale, when you breathe out.

You can also place a stuffy or doll on your belly and pretend it's riding a wave, going up and down.

Try this by yourself or with a buddy for three minutes.

Lion's Breath

You are always breathing. Though your breath flows in and out, it's always with you. You can control your breathing and return to it at any time. Remember you are working to make your brain stronger!

Steps

Get into a comfy position. I recommend sitting on a cushion, a chair, or criss-cross-applesauce on the floor. Just make sure you're comfortable.

Take a deep cleansing breath.

Look up at the ceiling.

Open your mouth as wide as you can.

Stick out your tongue as far as it will go, curling your tongue downward.

Exhale forcefully while making a "haaaa" sound.

Try this by yourself or with a buddy for three minutes.

Ocean Breath

You are always breathing. Though your breath flows in and out, it's always with you. You can control your breathing and return to it at any time. Ocean breath helps you focus and relax, and it makes your lungs stronger.

Steps

Come into a comfy seated position. You can sit in a chair, on a mat, or on a cushion. Just make sure you are comfortable.

Grab a mirror or glass and fog it up with your breath.

Call your attention to the hissing sound that your breath makes. It sounds sort of like the ocean. Do you hear it?

Close your mouth and see if you can make the same sound and sensation on both the inhale and exhale.

This breathing pattern helps to calm the body's fight-or-flight response. Try breathing this way for three minutes.

Chicken Breath

Chicken breath looks ridiculous, so don't be afraid to look silly! Make sure you keep your mouth closed during this activity so you don't become dizzy. This practice is great when you need a quick burst of energy.

Steps

Stand up and stretch.

Begin to take very quick, short, deep breaths in rapid succession.

Bend your arms and pump them up and down (like a bellow) while you breathe. Your arms should look like wings, but they shouldn't be loose or flappy. They should be strong.

Your arms should pump up as you inhale and should pump down as you exhale.

Begin to bend your knees as you exhale and straighten your knees as you inhale.

After two minutes, stop, close your eyes, and draw your attention back to your breath.

How does your body feel?

Feelings Wheel

How do you feel?

Author Amanda Lynch

Amanda Lynch, MA, CTP-E, RYT-200, is a trauma-informed specialist who is an expert in teacher self-care, student and family engagement, mindfulness-based trauma-informed practices, and restorative justice.

Amanda lives with her husband, Marcus, and her very busy children, Justin, Ava, Hazy, and Rosebud, in Glen Allen, Virginia.

She is the founder of Rethinking Resiliency LLC, a think tank of professionals who provide educational consulting and trauma-informed professional development services.

Author Hazy

Violet-Hazel (Hazy) Lynch is a first grade student in Richmond, Virginia. She likes to sing, dance, and play with her dog. She is full of energy and she is always in motion.

She wants to be a rockstar when she grows up. She lives with her parents, siblings, and dog in Glen Allen, Virginia.

Author Primrose

Primrose (Rosie) Lynch is a preschool student in Richmond, Virginia. She likes to run, jump, and play with dolls with her sister, Hazy. She also likes to watch Youtube videos.

She wants to be a comic book writer when she grows up. She lives with her parents, siblings, and dog in Glen Allen, Virginia.

ILLUSTRATOR BONNIE LEMAIRE

Award-winning illustrator Bonnie Lemaire began her career as a freelance illustrator with a promotional postcard in 1989. She is a graduate of Ontario College of Art's Communication and Design program, specializing in medical illustration. Her eternal optimism is the foundation of every drawing. Stillness and quirky behavior of those around her are a constant inspiration. Comical and curious characters and creatures come alive and dance on her pages, bringing smiles to small faces and delight to her readers all over the world.

Bonnie works in her home studio located in a small hamlet in Northern Ontario, Canada, surrounded by her loving family and her furry friend, Crowquill the studio cat, not to mention three quite lively hens cackling away in a converted backyard treehouse chicken coop.

Hall of Fame Backers

Genesis Beevas,
Samir and Saniyya Cusano,
Carl Davis, Jr., Carl Davis, Sr.,
Victoria and Jordynn Garrett,
Cailee and Cayden Parker,
Serenity L. Rose,
Rachelle Jones Smith,
RiAnne Smith,
Trinity Sophie Smith,
Aminta and Aniya Trepagnier

Made in the USA
Middletown, DE
13 March 2022